D1459600

D

For K & E and for Maxine, whose dad worked with lions – A.L.

For my dad! – L.B.

First published in 2014
by Scholastic Children's Books
Euston House, 24 Eversholt Street
London NW1 1DB
a division of Scholastic Ltd
www.scholastic.co.uk
London ~ New York ~ Toronto ~ Sydney ~ Auckland
Mexico City ~ New Delhi ~ Hong Kong

PB ISBN 978 1407 11564 1

Printed in Singapore

1 3 5 7 9 10 8 6 4 2

Papers used by Scholastic Children's Books are made from wood grown in sustainable forests.

SCHOLASTIC

COWBOYS WANTED
Dog Groomer Needed
TODAY'S JOBS
WANTED
WANT
Just the Job for Dad
Written by
Abie Longstaff
Illustrated by
Lauren Beard
WANTED
DINOSAUR HUNTER!
Large net supplied.
Haunted HouseKeeper
DO YOU HAVE SPIRIT?
CALL US TODAY!

Dad was rushing.

He ran back and forth across the kitchen

pulling on his socks,

pouring milk,

popping up toast and

packing his briefcase.

POP!
Emma
Sam

"You're busy this morning," said Emma.

"Why are you running around?" asked Sam.

"I'm **late** for work," Dad explained. "I have a meeting first thing, and I need to file a form. Then I have to type a report, and after lunch I have another meeting."

Emma and Sam

yawned.

Dad's job was **SO** boring.

"But then," said Dad, "I'll come home early and see **you!**"
He blew kisses as he waved goodbye.

The children looked at each other.
They had just had a **brilliant** idea.

"Let's find Dad a more exciting job," said Emma.

"Something fun," Sam added,
"somewhere amazing for us to visit."
"I know just where to start!"
Emma cried.

At the castle, **Sir Brave~a~Lot** and his knights were riding their horses.

"Excuse me please," Emma bowed.

"Good morrow, fair maiden," boomed Sir Brave-a-Lot. "Pray tell, what is thy quest?"

"Are there any jobs here for our dad?" Emma asked.

"Certainly!" said Sir Brave-a-Lot. "We need someone to tickle the dragon and distract him while we get the King's treasure back."

"**Perfect!**" cried Sam.

"That's **just the job** for Dad!"

"**Joyous news!**" Sir Brave-a-Lot cheered.
"Tell your dad we ride at sunrise!"

"Oh," said Emma.
"Oh," said Sam.

"Dad makes us breakfast every morning," Emma explained.

"He can't miss that," Sam cried.

"Verily he cannot," Sir Brave-a-Lot waved goodbye. "Fare thee well!"

"Come on Emma," Sam tugged her arm, "let's try the lagoon."

Down by the pier, **Captain Scratch-Beard** was washing his ship.

"Excuse me please," Sam waved hello.

"Ahoy there, me hearties!" called Captain Scratch-Beard. "What can I do for you?"

"Are there any jobs here for our dad?" asked Emma.

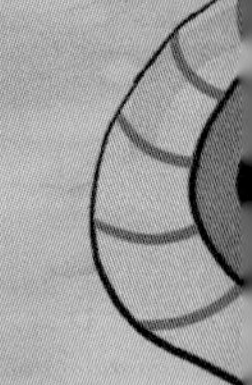

Captain Scratch-Beard scratched his beard,
"We do need someone to keep a look
out from the crow's nest."

"**Perfect!**" said Sam.
"That's **just the job** for Dad!"

"Arrrgh!" cheered the Captain.

"We sail at five o'clock. Tell yer dad to be here then."

"Oh," said Emma.

"Oh," said Sam.

"At five o'clock Dad takes us swimming," Emma explained.

"He can't miss that," Sam cried.

"Arr no, that he can't," Captain Scratch-Beard waved goodbye. "Farewell maties!"

"Let's try somewhere else," said Emma.

But the **tightrope walkers** always performed at **dinner** time.

The **jungle explorers** were leaving at **bath** time.

And the **wizard** cast spells at **midnight**, when the whole family would be tucked up in bed.

"There's one last place we could try!" Emma led the way.

At the space station, **Astro Annie** and her crew were setting up the rocket, ready to zoom into space.

"Excuse me please," Sam called.

"Reading you loud and clear," reported Annie, "How can I help?"

"Are there any jobs here for our dad?" asked Emma.

"Affirmative," Annie replied. "We need someone to fly the rocket to the moon."

"**Perfect!**" said Sam.

"That's **just the job** for Dad!"

"Roger that," Annie gave them the thumbs up. "He'll be in the pilot's seat for a week."

"A week?" said Emma.

"A whole week?" said Sam.

“But on **Mondays**
he picks us up
from school.”

“On **Wednesdays**
he takes us to the park.”

"On **Fridays**
he cooks dinner."

"**Every night**
he tucks us up in bed.
Then he reads us our
favourite stories."

"We'll miss him if we
don't see him," cried
the children.

"Understood," Annie waved.
"Good luck with your mission."

“Dad, we’ve decided you can **keep** your job,” said Emma.

“Yes,” Sam nodded. “You can go to meetings, you can file forms and you can type up reports, just as long as you still come home early and see us.”

Dad smiled, “Then that’s **just the job** for me!”

"Besides," added Emma, "we have enough excitement with Mum's job anyway...

…especially when she drops us at
school on her way to work!"
A1-MUM
RESCUE

SCHOOL

POLICE

PIZZA
PIZZA
PIZZA
PIZZA